TAKE HEART, MY CHILD

A MOTHER'S DREAM

AINSLEY EARHARDT

TAKE HEART,

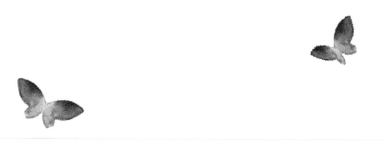

MY CHILD

A MOTHER'S DREAM

WITH KATHRYN CRISTALDI

ILLUSTRATED BY JAIME KIM

ALADDIN New York London Sydney New Delhi Toronto

Before you were born
Before you came to be
I dreamed a love song

On a butterfly sea.

The waters that day
Whispered truths in my ears
Of hopes for you, Love,
   for your life through the years.

May your feet trace new patterns
On warm, sandy shores
May you dive into waves
And yearn to explore.

But if you get lost
In the ocean's vast tides

Take heart, my child,
I'll be by your side.

Before you were born
Before you came to me
I dreamed a love song
By a polka-dot tree.

The leaves on the tree
Hummed an uplifting chord
Filled with poems for you, Love,
that could not be ignored.

May you never grow tired
Of stretching your branches
Dare to be different
Don't deny second chances.

And when winter comes
And leaves fall and fade
Take heart, my child,
Don't be afraid.

Before you were born
Before you shared my day
I dreamed a love song
Near a grand deer ballet.

The rocky foothills
Rumbled secrets, it's true
Gentle thoughts for this life
All directed at you.

May you take the high road
Though the road may be long
Pledge to follow your heart
So your heart will grow strong.

And if you stumble
Or the path grows too steep
Take heart, my child,
Trust yourself, take that leap.

Before you were born
Before you filled my hours
I dreamed a love song
By a moon made of flowers.

The stars lit the sky
With visions of gold
Laced with wishes for you
and your fate to unfold.

May you strive to be happy
Change your course if you're not
Embrace the world's colors
Colors others forgot.

But if you grow lonely
Or stars disappear
Take heart, my child,
I will always be near.

And before I woke up from this wondrous dream
Heaven rained drops of love, so it seemed.

Then I opened my eyes to a world soft and new
As my heart burst with pride at the promise . . .

of you!

"I have told you these things, so that in me you may have peace. In this world you will have trouble. But TAKE HEART! I have overcome the world."–John 16:33

THE STORY BEHIND THE STORY

I grew up in South Carolina with wonderful parents. My mother was an early childhood education teacher and had to leave the house for work very early each morning. Therefore, Dad always prepared breakfast for my sister, my brother, and me. Most mornings, he left a little note next to our cereal bowls with a quote, scripture, or poem. Those messages were instrumental in my life and helped me with many important decisions. Dad loved to quote Walt Disney: "I hope I'll never be afraid to fail," which is a constant reminder to never give up and always strive for your goals despite any challenges.

My dad also taught me about perspective. I can remember being a cheerleader in seventh grade and not making the squad the following year in eighth grade. I was upset, and my father told me something that changed my attitude and taught me a lesson that I still carry with me. He reminded me that I had already been given the chance to be a cheerleader in the prior year, and told me another girl probably needed that spot more than I did. He said God knew I could handle the rejection and would bless me in other ways. His wisdom taught me to look at the situation with new eyes.

These life lessons, and many others from my parents, have helped shape my life and inspired me to write this book. That, and the news that my husband and I were expecting a baby.

I hope *Take Heart, My Child* will remind children everywhere to "take heart": Enjoy your life, don't take it too seriously, do the right thing always, never be afraid to change your course, and love beyond measure.

The author is donating 6.7% of her advance, and 10% of any subsequent royalties (in each case net of agency fees) to Folds of Honor, an organization that provides scholarships and assistance to the spouses and children of fallen soldiers in service to America. Learn more at foldsofhonor.org.

ALADDIN · An imprint of Simon & Schuster Children's Publishing Division · 1230 Avenue of the Americas, New York, New York 10020 · First Aladdin hardcover edition November 2016 · Text copyright © 2016 by Ainsley Proctor · Illustrations copyright © 2016 by Jaime Kim · All rights reserved, including the right of reproduction in whole or in part in any form. · ALADDIN is a trademark of Simon & Schuster, Inc., and related logo is a registered trademark of Simon & Schuster, Inc. · For information about special discounts for bulk purchases, please contact Simon & Schuster Special Sales at 1-866-506-1949 or business@simonandschuster.com. · The Simon & Schuster Speakers Bureau can bring authors to your live event. For more information or to book an event contact the Simon & Schuster Speakers Bureau at 1-866-248-3049 or visit our website at www.simonspeakers.com. · Designed by Jessica Handelman · The illustrations for this book were rendered in watercolor and digitally. · The text of this book was set in MrsEaves. · Manufactured in the United States of America 1216 PCH · 10 9 8 7 6 5 4 3 · Library of Congress Control Number 2016936412 · ISBN 978-1-4814-6622-6 (hc) · ISBN 978-1-4814-6623-3 (eBook)